Soldier Bo

Michael Shaara

Alpha Editions

This edition published in 2023

ISBN : 9789357960960

Design and Setting By
Alpha Editions
www.alphaedis.com
Email - info@alphaedis.com

SOLDIER BOY

By MICHAEL SHAARA
Illustrated by EMSH

It's one thing to laugh at a man because his job is useless and outdated—another to depend on him when it suddenly isn't.

In the northland, deep, and in a great cave, by an everburning fire the Warrior sleeps. For this is the resting time, the time of peace, and so shall it be for a thousand years. And yet we shall summon him again, my children, when we are sore in need, and out of the north he will come, and again and again, each time we call, out of the dark and the cold, with the fire in his hands, he will come.

—Scandinavian legend

Throughout the night, thick clouds had been piling in the north; in the morning, it was misty and cold. By eight o'clock a wet, heavy, snow-smelling breeze had begun to set in, and because the crops were all down and the winter planting done, the colonists brewed hot coffee and remained inside. The wind blew steadily, icily from the north. It was well below freezing when, some time after nine, an army ship landed in a field near the settlement.

There was still time. There were some last brief moments in which the colonists could act and feel as they had always done. They therefore grumbled in annoyance. They wanted no soldiers here. The few who had convenient windows stared out with distaste and a mild curiosity, but no one went out to greet them.

After a while a rather tall, frail-looking man came out of the ship and stood upon the hard ground looking toward the village. He remained there, waiting stiffly, his face turned from the wind. It was a silly thing to do. He was obviously not coming in, either out of pride or just plain orneriness.

"Well, I never," a nice lady said.

"What's he just *standing* there for?" another lady said.

And all of them thought: well, God knows what's in the mind of a soldier, and right away many people concluded that he must be drunk. The seed of

- 1 -

peace was deeply planted in these people, in the children and the women, very, very deep. And because they had been taught, oh so carefully, to hate war they had also been taught, quite incidentally, to despise soldiers.

The lone man kept standing in the freezing wind.

Eventually, because even a soldier can look small and cold and pathetic, Bob Rossel had to get up out of a nice, warm bed and go out in that miserable cold to meet him.

The soldier saluted. Like most soldiers, he was not too neat and not too clean and the salute was sloppy. Although he was bigger than Rossel he did not seem bigger. And, because of the cold, there were tears gathering in the ends of his eyes.

"Captain Dylan, sir." His voice was low and did not carry. "I have a message from Fleet Headquarters. Are you in charge here?"

Rossel, a small sober man, grunted. "Nobody's in charge here. If you want a spokesman I guess I'll do. What's up?"

The captain regarded him briefly out of pale blue, expressionless eyes. Then he pulled an envelope from an inside pocket, handed it to Rossel. It was a thick, official-looking thing and Rossel hefted it idly. He was about to ask again what was it all about when the airlock of the hovering ship swung open creakily. A beefy, black-haired young man appeared unsteadily in the doorway, called to Dylan.

"C'n I go now, Jim?"

Dylan turned and nodded.

"Be back for you tonight," the young man called, and then, grinning, he yelled "Catch" and tossed down a bottle. The captain caught it and put it unconcernedly into his pocket while Rossel stared in disgust. A moment later the airlock closed and the ship prepared to lift.

"Was he *drunk*?" Rossel began angrily. "Was that a bottle of *liquor*?"

The soldier was looking at him calmly, coldly. He indicated the envelope in Rossel's hand. "You'd better read that and get moving. We haven't much time."

He turned and walked toward the buildings and Rossel had to follow. As Rossel drew near the walls the watchers could see his lips moving but could not hear him. Just then the ship lifted and they turned to watch that, and followed it upward, red spark-tailed, into the gray spongy clouds and the cold.

After a while the ship went out of sight, and nobody ever saw it again.

The first contact Man had ever had with an intelligent alien race occurred out on the perimeter in a small quiet place a long way from home. Late in the year 2360—the exact date remains unknown—an alien force attacked and destroyed the colony at Lupus V. The wreckage and the dead were found by a mailship which flashed off screaming for the army.

When the army came it found this: Of the seventy registered colonists, thirty-one were dead. The rest, including some women and children, were missing. All technical equipment, all radios, guns, machines, even books, were also missing. The buildings had been burned, so were the bodies. Apparently the aliens had a heat ray. What else they had, nobody knew. After a few days of walking around in the ash, one soldier finally stumbled on something.

For security reasons, there was a detonator in one of the main buildings. In case of enemy attack, Security had provided a bomb to be buried in the center of each colony, because it was important to blow a whole village to hell and gone rather than let a hostile alien learn vital facts about human technology and body chemistry. There was a bomb at Lupus V too, and though it had been detonated it had not blown. The detonating wire had been cut.

In the heart of the camp, hidden from view under twelve inches of earth, the wire had been dug up and cut.

The army could not understand it and had no time to try. After five hundred years of peace and anti-war conditioning the army was small, weak and without respect. Therefore, the army did nothing but spread the news, and Man began to fall back.

In a thickening, hastening stream he came back from the hard-won stars, blowing up his homes behind him, stunned and cursing. Most of the colonists got out in time. A few, the farthest and loneliest, died in fire before the army ships could reach them. And the men in those ships, drinkers and gamblers and veterans of nothing, the dregs of a society which had grown beyond them, were for a long while the only defense Earth had.

This was the message Captain Dylan had brought, come out from Earth with a bottle on his hip.

An obscenely cheerful expression upon his gaunt, not too well shaven face, Captain Dylan perched himself upon the edge of a table and listened, one long booted leg swinging idly. One by one the colonists were beginning to understand. War is huge and comes with great suddenness and always without reason, and there is inevitably a wait, between acts, between the news and the motion, the fear and the rage.

Dylan waited. These people were taking it well, much better than those in the cities had taken it. But then, these were pioneers. Dylan grinned. Pioneers. Before you settle a planet you boil it and bake it and purge it of all possible disease. Then you step down gingerly and inflate your plastic houses, which harden and become warm and impregnable; and send your machines out to plant and harvest; and set up automatic factories to transmute dirt into coffee; and, without ever having lifted a finger, you have braved the wilderness, hewed a home out of the living rock and become a pioneer. Dylan grinned again. But at least this was better than the wailing of the cities.

This Dylan thought, although he was himself no fighter, no man at all by any standards. This he thought because he was a soldier and an outcast; to every drunken man the fall of the sober is a happy thing. He stirred restlessly.

By this time the colonists had begun to realize that there wasn't much to say, and a tall, handsome woman was murmuring distractedly: "Lupus, Lupus—doesn't that mean wolves or something?"

Dylan began to wish they would get moving, these pioneers. It was very possible that the aliens would be here soon, and there was no need for discussion. There was only one thing to do and that was to clear the hell out, quickly and without argument. They began to see it.

But, when the fear had died down, the resentment came. A number of women began to cluster around Dylan and complain, working up their anger. Dylan said nothing. Then the man Rossel pushed forward and confronted him, speaking with a vast annoyance.

"See here, soldier, this is our planet. I mean to say, this is our *home*. We demand some protection from the fleet. By God, we've been paying the freight for you boys all these years and it's high time you earned your keep. We demand...."

It went on and on while Dylan looked at the clock and waited. He hoped that he could end this quickly. A big gloomy man was in front of him now and giving him that name of ancient contempt, "soldier boy." The gloomy man wanted to know where the fleet was.

"There is no fleet. There are a few hundred half-shot old tubs that were obsolete before you were born. There are four or five new jobs for the brass and the government. That's all the fleet there is."

Dylan wanted to go on about that, to remind them that nobody had wanted the army, that the fleet had grown smaller and smaller ... but this was not the time. It was ten-thirty already and the damned aliens might be coming in right now for all he knew, and all they did was talk. He had realized a long time ago that no peace-loving nation in the history of Earth had ever kept itself strong, and although peace was a noble dream, it was ended now and it was time to move.

"We'd better get going," he finally said, and there was quiet. "Lieutenant Bossio has gone on to your sister colony at Planet Three of this system. He'll return to pick me up by nightfall and I'm instructed to have you gone by then."

For a long moment they waited, and then one man abruptly walked off and the rest followed quickly; in a moment they were all gone. One or two stopped long enough to complain about the fleet, and the big gloomy man said he wanted guns, that's all, and there wouldn't nobody get him off his planet. When he left, Dylan breathed with relief and went out to check the bomb, grateful for the action.

Most of it had to be done in the open. He found a metal bar in the radio shack and began chopping at the frozen ground, following the wire. It was the first thing he had done with his hands in weeks, and it felt fine.

Dylan had been called up out of a bar—he and Bossio—and told what had happened, and in three weeks now they had cleared four colonies. This would be the last, and the tension here was beginning to get to him. After thirty years of hanging around and playing like the town drunk, a man could not be expected to rush out and plug the breach, just like that. It would take time.

He rested, sweating, took a pull from the bottle on his hip.

Before they sent him out on this trip they had made him a captain. Well, that was nice. After thirty years he was a captain. For thirty years he had bummed all over the west end of space, had scraped his way along the outer edges of Mankind, had waited and dozed and patrolled and got drunk, waiting always for something to happen. There were a lot of ways to pass the time while you waited for something to happen, and he had done them all.

Once he had even studied military tactics.

He could not help smiling at that, even now. Damn it, he'd been green. But he'd been only nineteen when his father died—of a hernia, of a crazy fool thing like a hernia that killed him just because he'd worked too long on a heavy planet—and in those days the anti-war conditioning out on the Rim was not very strong. They talked a lot about guardians of the frontier, and they got him and some other kids and a broken-down doctor. And ... now he was a captain.

He bent his back savagely, digging at the ground. You wait and you wait and the edge goes off. This thing he had waited for all those damn days was upon him now and there was nothing he could do but say the hell with it and go home. Somewhere along the line, in some dark corner of the bars or the jails, in one of the million soul-murdering insults which are reserved especially for peacetime soldiers, he had lost the core of himself, and it didn't particularly matter. That was the point: it made no particular difference if he never got it back. He owed nobody. He was tugging at the wire and trying to think of something pleasant from the old days, when the wire came loose in his hands.

Although he had been, in his cynical way, expecting it, for a moment it threw him and he just stared. The end was clean and bright. The wire had just been cut.

Dylan sat for a long while by the radio shack, holding the ends in his hands. He reached almost automatically for the bottle on his hip and then, for the first time he could remember, let it go. This was real, there was no time for that.

When Rossel came up, Dylan was still sitting. Rossel was so excited he did not notice the wire.

"Listen, soldier, how many people can your ship take?"

Dylan looked at him vaguely. "She sleeps two and won't take off with more'n ten. Why?"

His eyes bright and worried, Rossel leaned heavily against the shack. "We're overloaded. There are sixty of us and our ship will only take forty. We came out in groups, we never thought...."

Dylan dropped his eyes, swearing silently. "You're sure? No baggage, no iron rations; you couldn't get ten more on?"

"Not a chance. She's only a little ship with one deck—she's all we could afford."

Dylan whistled. He had begun to feel light-headed. "It 'pears that somebody's gonna find out first hand what them aliens look like."

It was the wrong thing to say and he knew it. "All right," he said quickly, still staring at the clear-sliced wire, "we'll do what we can. Maybe the colony on Three has room. I'll call Bossio and ask."

The colonist had begun to look quite pitifully at the buildings around him and the scurrying people.

"Aren't there any fleet ships within radio distance?"

Dylan shook his head. "The fleet's spread out kind of thin nowadays." Because the other was leaning on him he felt a great irritation, but he said, as kindly as he could, "We'll get 'em all out. One way or another, we won't leave anybody."

It was then that Rossel saw the wire. Thickly, he asked what had happened.

Dylan showed him the two clean ends. "Somebody dug it up, cut it, then buried it again and packed it down real nice."

"The damn fool!" Rossel exploded.

"Who?"

"Why, one of ... of us, of course. I know nobody ever liked sitting on a live bomb like this, but I never...."

"You think one of your people did it?"

Rossel stared at him. "Isn't that obvious?"

"Why?"

"Well, they probably thought it was too dangerous, and silly too, like most government rules. Or maybe one of the kids...."

It was then that Dylan told him about the wire on Lupus V. Rossel was silent. Involuntarily, he glanced at the sky, then he said shakily, "Maybe an animal?"

Dylan shook his head. "No animal did that. Wouldn't have buried it, or found it in the first place. Heck of a coincidence, don't you think? The wire at Lupus was cut just before an alien attack, and now this one is cut too— newly cut."

The colonist put one hand to his mouth, his eyes wide and white.

"So something," said Dylan, "knew enough about this camp to know that a bomb was buried here and also to know why it was here. And that something didn't want the camp destroyed and so came right into the center of the camp, traced the wire, dug it up and cut it. And then walked right out again."

"Listen," said Rossel, "I'd better go ask."

He started away but Dylan caught his arm.

"Tell them to arm," he said, "and try not to scare hell out of them. I'll be with you as soon as I've spliced this wire."

Rossel nodded and went off, running. Dylan knelt with the metal in his hands.

He began to feel that, by God, he was getting cold. He realized that he'd better go inside soon, but the wire had to be spliced. That was perhaps the most important thing he could do now, splice the wire.

All right, he asked himself for the thousandth time, who cut it? How? Telepathy? Could they somehow control one of us?

No. If they controlled one, then they could control all, and then there would be no need for an attack. But you don't know, you don't really know.

Were they small? Little animals?

Unlikely. Biology said that really intelligent life required a sizable brain and you would have to expect an alien to be at least as large as a dog. And every form of life on this planet had been screened long before a colony had been allowed in. If any new animals had suddenly shown up, Rossel would certainly know about it.

He would ask Rossel. He would damn sure have to ask Rossel.

He finished splicing the wire and tucked it into the ground. Then he straightened up and, before he went into the radio shack, he pulled out his pistol. He checked it, primed it, and tried to remember the last time he had fired it. He never had—he never had fired a gun.

The snow began falling near noon. There was nothing anybody could do but stand in the silence and watch it come down in a white rushing wall, and watch the trees and the hills drown in the whiteness, until there was nothing on the planet but the buildings and a few warm lights and the snow.

By one o'clock the visibility was down to zero and Dylan decided to try to contact Bossio again and tell him to hurry. But Bossio still didn't answer. Dylan stared long and thoughtfully out the window through the snow at the gray shrouded shapes of bushes and trees which were beginning to become horrifying. It must be that Bossio was still drunk—maybe sleeping it off before making planetfall on Three. Dylan held no grudge. Bossio was a kid and alone. It took a special kind of guts to take a ship out into space alone, when Things could be waiting....

A young girl, pink and lovely in a thick fur jacket, came into the shack and told him breathlessly that her father, Mr. Rush, would like to know if he wanted sentries posted. Dylan hadn't thought about it but he said yes right away, beginning to feel both pleased and irritated at the same time, because now they were coming to him.

He pushed out into the cold and went to find Rossel. With the snow it was bad enough, but if they were still here when the sun went down they wouldn't have a chance. Most of the men were out stripping down their ship and that would take a while. He wondered why Rossel hadn't yet put a call through to Three, asking about room on the ship there. The only answer he could find was that Rossel knew that there was no room, and he wanted to put off the answer as long as possible. And, in a way, you could not blame him.

Rossel was in his cabin with the big, gloomy man—who turned out to be Rush, the one who had asked about sentries. Rush was methodically cleaning an old hunting rifle. Rossel was surprisingly full of hope.

"Listen, there's a mail ship due in, been due since yesterday. We might get the rest of the folks out on that."

Dylan shrugged. "Don't count on it."

"But they have a contract!"

The soldier grinned.

The big man, Rush, was paying no attention. Quite suddenly he said: "Who cut that wire, Cap?"

Dylan swung slowly to look at him. "As far as I can figure, an alien cut it."

Rush shook his head. "No. Ain't been no aliens near this camp, and no peculiar animals either. We got a planet-wide radar, and ain't no unidentified ships come near, not since we first landed more'n a year ago." He lifted the rifle and peered through the bore. "Uh-uh. One of us did it."

The man had been thinking. And he knew the planet.

"Telepathy?" asked Dylan.

"Might be."

"Can't see it. You people live too close, you'd notice right away if one of you wasn't ... himself. And, if they've got one, why not all?"

Rush calmly—at least outwardly calmly—lit his pipe. There was a strength in this man that Dylan had missed before.

"Don't know," he said gruffly. "But these are aliens, mister. And until I know different I'm keepin' an eye on my neighbor."

He gave Rossel a sour look and Rossel stared back, uncomprehending.

Then Rossel jumped. "My God!"

Dylan moved to quiet him. "Look, is there any animal at all that ever comes near here that's as large as a dog?"

After a pause, Rush answered. "Yep, there's one. The viggle. It's like a reg'lar monkey but with four legs. Biology cleared 'em before we landed. We shoot one now and then when they get pesky." He rose slowly, the rifle held under his arm. "I b'lieve we might just as well go post them sentries."

Dylan wanted to go on with this but there was nothing much else to say. Rossel went with them as far as the radio shack, with a strained expression on his face, to put through that call to Three.

When he was gone Rush asked Dylan, "Where you want them sentries? I got Walt Halloran and Web Eggers and six others lined up."

Dylan stopped and looked around grimly at the circling wall of snow. "You know the site better than I do. Post 'em in a ring, on rises, within calling distance. Have 'em check with each other every five minutes. I'll go help your people at the ship."

The gloomy man nodded and fluffed up his collar. "Nice day for huntin'," he said, and then he was gone with the snow quickly covering his footprints.

The Alien lay wrapped in a thick electric cocoon, buried in a wide warm room beneath the base of a tree. The tree served him as antennae; curiously he gazed into a small view-screen and watched the humans come. He saw them fan out, eight of them, and sink down in the snow. He saw that they were armed.

He pulsed thoughtfully, extending a part of himself to absorb a spiced lizard. Since the morning, when the new ship had come, he had been watching steadily, and now it was apparent that the humans were aware of their danger. Undoubtedly they were preparing to leave.

That was unfortunate. The attack was not scheduled until late that night and he could not, of course, press the assault by day. But *flexibility*, he reminded himself sternly, *is the first principle of absorption*, and therefore he moved to alter his plans. A projection reached out to dial several knobs on a large box before him, and the hour of assault was moved forward to dusk. A glance at the chronometer told him that it was already well into the night on Planet Three, and that the attack there had probably begun.

The Alien felt the first tenuous pulsing of anticipation. He lay quietly, watching the small square lights of windows against the snow, thanking the

Unexplainable that matters had been so devised that he would not have to venture out into that miserable cold.

Presently an alarming thought struck him. These humans moved with uncommon speed for intelligent creatures. Even without devices, it was distinctly possible that they could be gone before nightfall. He could take no chance, of course. He spun more dials and pressed a single button, and lay back again comfortably, warmly, to watch the disabling of the colonists' ship.

When Three did not answer, Rossel was nervously gazing at the snow, thinking of other things, and he called again. Several moments later the realization of what was happening struck him like a blow. Three had never once failed to answer. All they had to do when they heard the signal buzz was go into the radio shack and say hello. That was all they had to do. He called again and again, but nobody answered. There was no static and no interference and he didn't hear a thing. He checked frenziedly through his own apparatus and tried again, but the air was as dead as deep space. He raced out to tell Dylan.

Dylan accepted it. He had known none of the people on Three and what he felt now was a much greater urgency to be out of here. He said hopeful things to Rossel, and then went out to the ship and joined the men in lightening her. About the ship at least, he knew something and he was able to tell them what partitions and frames could go and what would have to stay or the ship would never get off the planet. But even stripped down, it couldn't take them all. When he knew that, he realized that he himself would have to stay here, for it was only then that he thought of Bossio.

Three was dead. Bossio had gone down there some time ago and, if Three was dead and Bossio had not called, then the fact was that Bossio was gone too. For a long, long moment Dylan stood rooted in the snow. More than the fact that he would have to stay here was the unspoken, unalterable, heart-numbing knowledge that Bossio was dead—the one thing that Dylan could not accept. Bossio was the only friend he had. In all this dog-eared, aimless, ape-run Universe Bossio was all his friendship and his trust.

He left the ship blindly and went back to the settlement. Now the people were quiet and really frightened, and some of the women were beginning to cry. He noticed now that they had begun to look at him with hope as he passed, and in his own grief, humanly, he swore.

Bossio—a big-grinning kid with no parents, no enemies, no grudges— Bossio was already dead because he had come out here and tried to help these people. People who had kicked or ignored him all the days of his life.

And, in a short while, Dylan would also stay behind and die to save the life of somebody he never knew and who, twenty-four hours earlier, would have been ashamed to be found in his company. Now, when it was far, far too late, they were coming to the army for help.

But in the end, damn it, he could not hate these people. All they had ever wanted was peace, and even though they had never understood that the Universe is unknowable and that you must always have big shoulders, still they had always sought only for peace. If peace leads to no conflict at all and then decay, well, that was something that had to be learned. So he could not hate these people.

But he could not help them either. He turned from their eyes and went into the radio shack. It had begun to dawn on the women that they might be leaving without their husbands or sons, and he did not want to see the fierce struggle that he was sure would take place. He sat alone and tried, for the last time, to call Bossio.

After a while, an old woman found him and offered him coffee. It was a very decent thing to do, to think of him at a time like this, and he was so suddenly grateful he could only nod. The woman said that he must be cold in that thin army thing and that she had brought along a mackinaw for him. She poured the coffee and left him alone.

They were thinking of him now, he knew, because they were thinking of everyone who had to stay. Throw the dog a bone. Dammit, don't be like that, he told himself. He had not had anything to eat all day and the coffee was warm and strong. He decided he might be of some help at the ship.

It was stripped down now and they were loading. He was startled to see a great group of them standing in the snow, removing their clothes. Then he understood. The clothes of forty people would change the weight by enough to get a few more aboard. There was no fighting. Some of the women were almost hysterical and a few had refused to go and were still in their cabins, but the process was orderly. Children went automatically, as did the youngest husbands and all the women. The elders were shuffling around in the snow, waving their arms to keep themselves warm. Some of them were laughing to keep their spirits up.

In the end, the ship took forty-six people.

Rossel was one of the ones that would not be going. Dylan saw him standing by the airlock holding his wife in his arms, his face buried in her soft brown hair. A sense of great sympathy, totally unexpected, rose up in Dylan, and a little of the lostness of thirty years went slipping away. These were his people. It was a thing he had never understood before, because he had never once been among men in great trouble. He waited and watched, learning, trying to digest this while there was still time. Then the semi-naked colonists were inside and the airlock closed. But when the ship tried to lift, there was a sharp burning smell—she couldn't get off the ground.

Rush was sitting hunched over in the snow, his rifle across his knees. He was coated a thick white and if he hadn't spoken Dylan would have stumbled over him. Dylan took out his pistol and sat down.

"What happened?" Rush asked.

"Lining burned out. She's being repaired."

"Coincidence?"

Dylan shook his head.

"How long'll it take to fix?"

"Four—five hours."

"It'll be night by then." Rush paused. "I wonder."

"Seems like they want to wait 'til dark."

"That's what I was figurin'. Could be they ain't got much of a force."

Dylan shrugged. "Also could mean they see better at night. Also could mean they move slow. Also could mean they want the least number of casualties."

Rush was quiet and the snow fell softly on his face, on his eyebrows, where it had begun to gather. At length he said, "You got any idea how they got to the ship?"

Dylan shook his head again. "Nobody saw anything—but they were all pretty busy. Your theory about it maybe being one of us is beginning to look pretty good."

The colonist took off his gloves, lit a cigarette. The flame was strong and piercing and Dylan moved to check him, but stopped. It didn't make much difference. The aliens knew where they were.

And this is right where we're gonna be, he thought.

"You know," he said suddenly, speaking mostly to himself, "I been in the army thirty years, and this is the first time I was ever in a fight. Once in a while we used to chase smugglers—never caught any, their ships were new—used to cut out after unlicensed ships, used to do all kinds of piddling things like that. But I never shot at anybody."

Rush was looking off into the woods. "Maybe the mail ship will come in."

Dylan nodded.

"They got a franchise, dammit. They got to deliver as long as they's a colony here."

When Dylan didn't answer, he said almost appealingly: "Some of those guys would walk barefoot through hell for a buck."

"Maybe," Dylan said. After all, why not let him hope? There were four long hours left.

Now he began to look down into himself, curiously, because he himself was utterly without hope and yet he was no longer really afraid. It was a surprising thing when you looked at it coldly, and he guessed that, after all, it was because of the thirty years. A part of him had waited for this. Some crazy part of him was ready—even after all this time—even excited about being in a fight. Well, what the hell, he marveled. And then he realized that the rest of him was awakening too, and he saw that this job was really his ... that he had always been, in truth, a soldier.

Dylan sat, finding himself in the snow. Once long ago he had read about some fool who didn't want to die in bed, old and feeble. This character wanted to reach the height of his powers and then explode in a grand way—"in Technicolor," the man had said. Explode in Technicolor. It was meant to be funny, of course, but he had always remembered it, and he realized now that that was a small part of what he was feeling. The rest of it was that he was a soldier.

Barbarian, said a small voice, *primitive*. But he couldn't listen.

"Say, Cap," Rush was saying, "it's getting a mite chilly. I understand you got a bottle."

"Sure," he said cheerfully, "near forgot it." He pulled it out and gave it to Rush. The colonist broke the seal and drank, saying to Dylan half-seriously, half-humorously: "One for the road."

Beneath them the planet revolved and the night came on. They waited, speaking briefly, while the unseen sun went down. And faintly, dimly through the snow, they heard at last the muffled beating of a ship. It passed overhead and they were sighting their guns before they recognized it. It was the mailship.

They listened while she settled in a field by the camp, and Rush was pounding Dylan's arm. "She will take us all," Rush was shouting, "she'll take us all," and Dylan too was grinning, and then he saw a thing.

Small and shadowy, white-coated and almost invisible, the thing had come out of the woods and was moving toward them, bobbing and shuffling in the silent snow.

Dylan fired instinctively, because the thing had four arms and was coming right at him. He fired again. This time he hit it and the thing fell, but almost immediately it was up and lurching rapidly back into the trees. It was gone before Dylan could fire again.

They both lay flat in the snow, half-buried. From the camp there were now no sounds at all. For the first time today Dylan could hear the snow fall.

"Did you get a good look?"

Rush grunted, relaxing. "Should've saved your fire, son. Looked like one o' them monkeys."

But there was something wrong. There was something that Dylan had heard in the quickness of the moment which he could not remember but which was very wrong.

"Listen," he said, suddenly placing it. "Dammit, that was no monkey."

"Easy—"

"I hit it. I hit it cold. It made a *noise*."

Rush was staring at him.

"Didn't you hear?" Dylan cried.

"No. Your gun was by my ear."

And then Dylan was up and running, hunched over, across the snow to where the thing had fallen. He had seen a piece of it break off when the bolt struck, and now in the snow he picked up a paw and brought it back to Rush. He saw right away there was no blood. The skin was real and furry all right but there was no blood. Because the bone was steel and the muscles were springs and the thing had been a robot.

The Alien rose up from his cot, whistling with annoyance. When that ship had come in, his attention had been distracted from one of the robots, and of course the miserable thing had gone blundering right out into the humans. He thought for a while that the humans would overlook it—the seeing was poor and they undoubtedly would still think of it as animal, even with its firing ports open—but then he checked the robot and saw that a piece was missing and knew that the humans had found it. Well, he thought unhappily, flowing into his suit, no chance now to disable that other ship. The humans would never let another animal near.

And therefore—for he was, above all, a flexible being—he would proceed to another plan. The settlement would have to be detonated. And for that he would have to leave his own shelter and go out in that miserable cold and lie down in one of his bunkers which was much farther away. No need to risk blowing himself up with his own bombs, but still, that awful cold.

He dismissed his regrets and buckled his suit into place. It carried him up the stairs and bore him out into the snow. After one whiff of the cold, he snapped his viewplate shut and immediately, as he had expected, it began to film with snow. Well, no matter, he would guide the unit by coordinates and it would find the bunker itself. No need for caution now. The plan was nearly ended.

In spite of his recent setback, the Alien lay back and allowed himself the satisfaction of a full tremble. The plan had worked very nearly to perfection, as of course it should, and he delighted in the contemplation of it.

When the humans were first detected, in the region of Bootes, much thought had gone into the proper method of learning their technology without being discovered themselves. There was little purpose in destroying the humans without first learning from them. Life was really a remarkable thing—one never knew what critical secrets a star-borne race possessed. Hence the robots. And it was an extraordinary plan, an elegant plan. The Alien trembled again.

The humans were moving outward toward the Rim, their base was apparently somewhere beyond Centaurus. Therefore, a ring of defense was thrown up on most of the habitable worlds toward which the humans were coming—oh, a delightful plan—and the humans came down one by one and never realized that there was any defense at all.

With a cleverness which was almost excruciating, the Aliens had carefully selected a number of animals native to each world, and then constructed robot duplicates. So simple then to place the robots down on a world with a single Director, then wait ... for the humans to inhabit. Naturally the humans screened all the animals and scouted a planet pretty thoroughly before they set up a colony. Naturally their snares and their hunters caught no robots, and never found the deep-buried Alien Director.

Then the humans relaxed and began to make homes, never realizing that in among the animals which gamboled playfully in the trees there was one which did not gambol, but watched. Never once noticing the monkey-like animals or the small thing like a rabbit which was a camera eye, or the thing like a rat which took chemical samples, or the thing like a lizard which cut wires.

The Alien rumbled on through the snow, trembling so much now with ecstasy and anticipation that the suit which bore him almost lost its balance. He very nearly fell over before he stopped trembling, and then he contained himself. In a little while, a very little while, there would be time enough for trembling.

"They could've been here 'til the sun went out," Rush said, "and we never would've known."

"I wonder how much they've found out," Dylan said.

Rush was holding the paw.

"Pretty near everything, I guess. This stuff don't stop at monkeys. Could be any size, any kind ... look, let's get down into camp and tell 'em."

Dylan rose slowly to a kneeling position, peering dazedly out into the far white trees. His mind was turning over and over, around and around, like a roulette wheel. But, at the center of his mind, there was one thought, and it was rising up slowly now, through the waste and waiting of the years. He felt a vague surprise.

"Gettin' kind of dark," he said.

Rush swore. "Let's go. Let's get out of here." He tugged once at Dylan's arm and started off on his knees.

Dylan said: "Wait."

Rush stopped. Through the snow he tried to see Dylan's eyes. The soldier was still looking into the woods.

Dylan's voice was halting and almost inaudible. "They know everything about us. We don't know anything about them. They're probably sittin' out there right now, a swarm of 'em there behind those trees, waitin' for it to get real nice and dark."

He paused. "If I could get just one."

It was totally unexpected, to Dylan as well as Rush. The time for this sort of thing was past, the age was done, and for a long while neither of them fully understood.

"C'mon," Rush said with exasperation.

Dylan shook his head, marveling at himself. "I'll be with you in a little while."

Rush came near and looked questioningly into his face.

"Listen," Dylan said hurriedly, "we only need one. If we could just get one back to a lab we'd at least have some clue to what they are. This way we don't know anything. We can't just cut and run." He struggled with the unfamiliar, time-lost words. "We got to make a stand."

He turned from Rush and lay forward on his belly in the snow. He could feel his heart beating against the soft white cushion beneath him. There was no time to look at this calmly and he was glad of that. He spent some time being very much afraid of the unknown things beyond the trees, but even then he realized that this was the one thing in his life he had to do.

It is not a matter of dying, he thought, but of *doing*. Sooner or later a man must do a thing which justifies his life, or the life is not worth living. The long cold line of his existence had reached this point, here and now in the snow at this moment. He would go on from here as a man ... or not at all.

Rush had sat down beside him, beginning to understand, watching without words. He was an old man. Like all Earthmen, he had never fought with his hands. He had not fought the land, or the tides, or the weather, or any of the million bitter sicknesses which Man had grown up fighting, and he was beginning to realize that somewhere along the line he had been betrayed. Now, with a dead paw of the enemy in his hand, he did not feel like a man. And he was ready to fight now, but it was much too late and he saw with a vast leaden shame that he did not know how, could not even begin.

"Can I help?" he said.

Dylan shook his head. "Go back and let them know about the robots, and, if the ship is ready to leave before I get back, well—then good luck."

He started to slither forward on his belly but Rush reached out and grabbed him, holding with one hand to peace and gentleness and the soft days which were ending.

"Listen," he said, "you don't owe anybody."

Dylan stared at him with surprise. "I know," he said, and then he slipped up over the mound before him and headed for the trees.

Now what he needed was luck. Just good, plain old luck. He didn't know where they were or how many there were or what kinds there were, and the chances were good that one of them was watching him right now. Well, then he needed some luck. He inched forward slowly, carefully, watching the oncoming line of trees. The snow was falling on him in big, leafy flakes and that was fine, because the blackness of his suit was much too distinct and the more white he was the better. Even so, it was becoming quite dark by now and he thought he had a chance. He reached the first tree.

Silently he slipped off his heavy cap. The visor got in his way and above all he must be able to see. He let the snow thicken on his hair before he raised himself on his elbows and looked outward.

There was nothing but the snow and the dead quiet and the stark white boles of the trees. He slid past the first trunk to the next, moving forward on his elbows with his pistol in his right hand. His elbow struck a rock and it hurt and his face was freezing. Once he rubbed snow from his eyebrows. Then he came through the trees and lay down before a slight rise, thinking.

Better to go around than over. But if anything is watching, it is most likely watching from above.

Therefore, go around and come back up from behind. Yes.

His nose had begun to run. With great care he crawled among some large rocks, hoping against hope that he would not sneeze. Why had nothing seen him? Was something following him now? He turned to look behind him but it was darker now and becoming difficult to see. But he would have to look behind him more often.

He was moving down a gorge. There were large trees above him and he needed their shelter, but he could not risk slipping down the sides of the gorge. And far off, weakly, out of the gray cold ahead, he heard a noise.

He lay face down in the snow, listening. With a slow, thick shuffle, a thing was moving through the trees before him. In a moment he saw that it was not coming toward him. He lifted his head but saw nothing. Much more slowly now, he crawled again. The thing was moving down the left side of the gorge ahead, coming away from the rise he had circled. It was moving without caution and he worried that if he did not hurry, he would lose it. But for the life of him he couldn't stand up.

The soldier went forward on his hands and knees. When his clothes hung down, the freezing cold entered his throat and shocked his body, which was sweating. He shifted his gun to his gloved hand and blew on the bare fingers of his right, still crawling. When he reached the other end of the gorge, he stood upright against a rock wall and looked in the direction of the shuffling thing.

He saw it just as it turned. It was a great black lump on a platform. The platform had legs and the thing was plodding methodically upon a path which would bring it past him. It had come down from the rise and was rounding the gorge when Dylan saw it. It did not see him.

If he had not ducked quickly and brought up his gun, the monkey would not have seen him either, but there was no time for regret. The monkey was several yards to the right of the lump on the platform when he heard it start running, and he had to look up this time and saw it leaping toward him over the snow.

All right, he said to himself. His first shot took the monkey in the head, where the eyes were. As the thing crashed over, there was a hiss and a stench, and flame seared into his shoulder and the side of his face. He lurched to the side, trying to see, his gun at arm's-length as the lump on the platform spun toward him. He fired four times. Three bolts went home in the lump, the fourth tore a leg off the platform and the whole thing fell over.

Dylan crawled painfully behind a rock, his left arm useless. The silence had come back again and he waited, but neither of the alien things moved. Nothing else moved in the woods around him. He turned his face up to the falling snow and let it come soothingly upon the awful wound in his side.

After a while he looked out at the monkey. It had risen to a sitting position but was frozen in the motion of rising. It had ceased to function when he hit the lump. Out of the numbness and the pain, he felt a great gladness rising.

The guide. He had killed the guide.

He would not be cautious any more. Maybe some of the other robots were self-directing and dangerous, but they could be handled. He went to the lump, stared at it without feeling. A black doughy bulge was swelling out through one of the holes.

It was too big to carry, but he would have to take something back. He went over and took the monkey by a stiff jutting arm and began dragging it back toward the village.

Now he began to stumble. It was dark and he was very tired. But the steel he had been forging in his breast was complete, and the days which were coming would be days full of living. He would walk with big shoulders and he would not bother to question, because Man was not born to live out his days at home, by the fire.

It was a very big thing that Dylan had learned and he could not express it, but he knew it all the same, knew it beyond understanding. And so he went home to his people.

One by one, increasing, in the wee black corner of space which Man had taken for his own, other men were learning. And the snow fell and the planets whirled, and, when it was spring where Dylan had fought, men were already leaping back out to the stars.

Milton Keynes UK
Ingram Content Group UK Ltd.
UKHW010839190424
441445UK00004B/332

9 789357 960960